WHY IS MOM SO MAD?

A BOOK ABOUT PTSD AND MILITARY FAMILIES

BY SETH and JULIA KASTLE

ILLUSTRATED BY KARISSA GONZALEZ-OTHON

Copyright © 2015 by Seth Kastle
All rights reserved.
Published by Kastle Books 700 Easter Ave
Wakeeney, KS 67672
All associated logos are trademark of
Kastle Books

2015

ISBN 9780692484494

www.KastleBooks.com

THIS BOOK IS DEDICATED TO THE MEMORY OF
CW2 BRYAN J. NICHOLS.

BRYAN, YOU WERE THE BEST OF US AND YOU ARE MISSED DAILY
AS A HUSBAND, FATHER, SON, BROTHER, AND FRIEND. THANK
YOU FOR BEING THE MOST AMAZING PERSON WE HAVE EVER BEEN
FORTUNATE ENOUGH TO KNOW.

LOVE, SETH AND JULIA

—WITH IT OR ON IT—

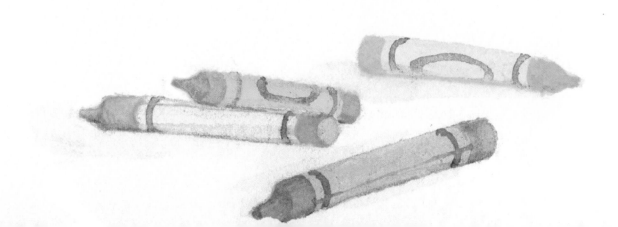

DAD, WHY IS MOM SO **MAD**

ALL THE TIME?

SHE WAS **MAD** AT ME TODAY FOR
SQUEEZING TOOTHPASTE ALL
OVER THE SINK.

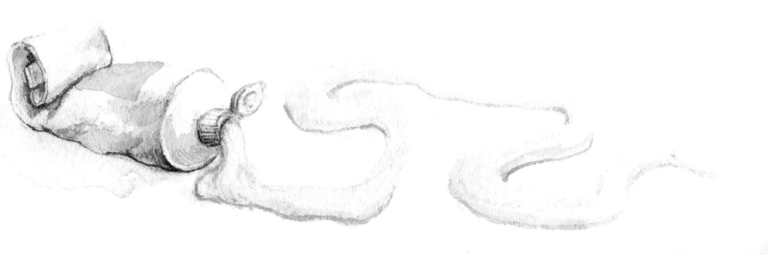

SHE WAS **MAD** AT ME THIS MORNING FOR WHINING.

SHE WAS **MAD** AT ME IN THE CAR FOR FIGHTING WITH MY BROTHER.

MOM WAS DIFFERENT WHEN SHE CAME
HOME FROM OVERSEAS. WHILE SHE
WAS AWAY SHE HAD TO DO A LOT OF

REALLY HARD,
DANGEROUS WORK,
AND IT MADE HER DIFFERENT THAN SHE USED TO BE.

MOM USED TO BE VERY CALM AND
WOULD NEVER GET **MAD**, BUT NOW
SHE HAS TROUBLE CONCENTRATING OR
BEING PATIENT.

NOW SHE GETS **ANGRY** FAST.

IT'S LIKE MOM ALWAYS HAS A
VOLCANO INSIDE HER,

AND WHEN SHE GETS MAD
THE PRESSURE

GROWS AND GROWS REALLY QUICKLY.

WHEN SHE GETS **MAD** IT'S LIKE THE VOLCANO IS **EXPLODING.**

WHEN MOM YELLS AND IS **MAD** IT'S NOT BECAUSE SHE WANTS TO MAKE YOU FEEL **SAD**. SHE WOULD DO ANYTHING NOT TO BE THE WAY SHE IS, BUT THE VOLCANO IS PART OF WHO SHE IS NOW.

SOMETIMES MOM CAN'T SLEEP, OR HAS BAD DREAMS. THIS MAKES HER UPSET TOO.

SOMETIMES MOM HAS A REALLY HARD TIME
REMEMBERING THINGS, WHICH MAKES IT HARD FOR
HER TO WORK.

AND HARD FOR HER TO
BE A MOM AND WIFE.

SOMETIMES MOM NEEDS SOME TIME ALONE TO LET THE **VOLCANO COOL**, OR JUST CLEAR HER MIND.

MOM **LOVES** YOU MORE THAN ANYTHING
IN THE WORLD.

JUST BECAUSE SHE GETS **MAD** EASILY IT DOESN'T MEAN SHE DOESN'T **CARE** ABOUT YOUR FEELINGS.

THINK ABOUT ALL THE TIMES MOM PLAYS WITH YOU.

THINK OF ALL THE FUN
THINGS YOU AND YOUR MOM
DO TOGETHER.

MOM AND DAD SOMETIMES FIGHT A LOT
NOW, BUT WE STILL

LOVE EACH OTHER.

SINCE WE ARE A MILITARY FAMILY WE ARE DIFFERENT THAN OTHER FAMILIES.

SOMETIMES MOM IS GONE A LOT AND THAT IS
SOMETHING THAT IS HARD FOR ALL OF US.

WE ALL GET **UPSET** SOMETIMES WHEN THINGS AREN'T THE WAY WE WOULD LIKE THEM TO BE.

MOM JUST HAS A REALLY SHORT
FUSE NOW AND CAN'T ALWAYS
BE OK WITH THE NORMAL
HICCUPS IN LIFE.

JUST KNOW THAT BOTH MOM AND DAD

LOVE

YOU AND EACH OTHER MORE THAN
ANYTHING.

SOMETIMES LIFE ISN'T PERFECT, BUT
WE ARE A FAMILY AND WE WILL STICK
TOGETHER AND

LOVE

EACH OTHER FOREVER.

SETH KASTLE IS THE AUTHOR OF THE CHILDREN'S BOOK WHY IS DAD SO MAD? AND WHY IS MOM SO MAD?. BOTH OF THESE BOOKS WERE WRITTEN IN ORDER TO ASSIST MILITARY FAMILIES WHO ARE STRUGGLING WITH PTSD.

SETH RETIRED AFTER A 16 YEAR MILITARY CAREER AS A COMPANY FIRST SERGEANT. HE WAS DEPLOYED IN JANUARY 2002 TO QATAR, AND THEN TO AFGHANISTAN FOR A TOTAL OF EIGHT MONTHS. HE WAS THEN DEPLOYED TO IRAQ IN JANUARY 2003 UNTIL APRIL 2004. HE HAS BEEN MARRIED SINCE 2005 TO HIS WIFE JULIA, AND HAS TWO DAUGHTERS: RAEGAN AND KENNEDY. HE WROTE THE BOOK WHY IS DAD SO MAD? TO TRY TO HELP HIS CHILDREN UNDERSTAND WHY HE IS THE WAY HE IS NOW. THE OVERRIDING PURPOSE OF THESE BOOKS IS TO LET CHILDREN OF SERVICE MEMBERS KNOW THAT NO MATTER WHAT, THEIR PARENTS LOVE THEM MORE THAN ANYTHING, DESPITE THE CHALLENGES THAT ARE FACED. SETH RESIDES IN KANSAS WHERE HE IS A PROFESSOR OF LEADERSHIP STUDIES AT FORT HAYS STATE UNIVERSITY.

JULIA KASTLE IS THE CO-AUTHOR OF THE CHILDREN'S BOOK WHY IS MOM SO MAD? SHE WROTE THIS BOOK TO HELP MILITARY FAMILIES IN WHICH THE MOTHER STRUGGLES WITH PTSD. JULIA ENDED HER TIME IN SERVICE AFTER SERVING 8 YEARS IN THE ARMY RESERVE AT THE RANK OF SERGEANT.

DURING HER TIME IN SERVICE SHE DEPLOYED TO QATAR IN 2002, AND IRAQ IN 2003 UNTIL APRIL OF 2004. SHE HAS BEEN MARRIED SINCE 2005 AND HAS TWO DAUGHTERS, RAEGAN AND KENNEDY. BY TRADE SHE IS A SONOGRAPHER, BUT IS CURRENTLY STAYING AT HOME WITH HER YOUNG CHILDREN. SHE UNDERSTANDS THE STRUGGLES MOTHERS WITH PTSD FACE, AND WISHES TO HELP THEM, AND HELP THEIR CHILDREN UNDERSTAND.

MORE INFORMATION CAN BE FOUND AT WWW.KASTLEBOOKS.COM.

Made in the USA
Columbia, SC
12 August 2019